THE FIRST THOUSAND WORDS IN SPANISH

With Easy Pronunciation Guide

Heather Amery and Reyes Milá

Illustrated by Stephen Cartwright

Pronunciation Guide by Judy Klavans, MED, MA

La casa

el baño

el jabón

el grifo

la espuma
de baño

el cepillo
de dientes

el agua

la toalla

la esponja

la ducha

la pasta
de dientes

el lavabo

el retrete

la biblioteca

la mesita

la radio

el radiador

la lana

el papel pintado

el reloj

la alfombra

el cojín

el tocadiscos

4

la lámpara

la cama

la cómoda

el cepillo

la almohada

el guardarropa

la alfombrilla

los cuadros

el edredón

los vestidos

el peine

el espejo

la sábana

las escaleras

la araña

la silla

las cartas

el teléfono

la telaraña

la mosca

el colgador de ropa

el periódico

5

En la cocina

la nevera

los vasos

el reloj

las cucharas
de madera

el delantal

el interruptor

las cacerolas

los platitos

la plancha

el calentador
de agua

el fregasuelos

el aspirador

el fregadero

los tenedores

la puerta

el trapo

el taburete

los cuchillos

la cera de lustre

6

la cocina

los azulejos

el cajón

la basura

la sartén

la lavadora

el recogedor del polvo

los platos

la tabla de planchar

el detergente

el cepillo

la mesa

la bombilla

las tazas

las cucharas

las cerillas

la llave

la escoba

las escudillas

el armario

En el jardín

la carretilla

la colmena

el caracol

los ladrillos

el cubo de basura

la oruga

la pala

la hormiga

el pájaro

el canalón del tejado

la escalera de mano

las semillas

el cobertizo

el gusano

las flores

el irrigador

el hueso

el seto

la paleta

8

el cortacésped

el camino

el árbol

la horca

las hojas

la escoba

la manguera

la azada

el humo

la abeja

el rastrillo

el cochecito de niño

la avispa

las plantas

la hierba

la hoguera

el nido de pájaro

los palos

el invernadero

9

El taller

el papel de lija

el taladro

los tornillos a tuerca

las tachuelas

la sierra

el serrín

el martillo

la lima

la caja de herramientas

el destornillador

el tablón

el bote de pintura

las virutas

la navaja

10

el barril

el hacha

las tuercas

la cinta
de medir

los tornillos

la escalera
de mano

los clavos

el torno
de banco

la leña

el banco

los potes

la madera

el
cepillo
de carpintero

11

La calle

la gasolinera

la ambulancia

la bicicleta

el agujero

el bar

la acera

la tienda

el semáforo

la chimenea

el camión

el paso de peatones

los escalones

el hombre

el hotel

el coche de policía

la apisonadora

la taladradora

la escuela

el patio de recreo

los pisos

12

la estatua

el autobús

el taxi

el remolque

las tuberías

el tejado

el mercado

la fábrica

la antena
de televisión

la furgoneta

el policía

el coche de
bomberos

la casa

la mujer

excavadora

la iglesia

el cine

el coche

la
motocicleta

el conductor

el farol

13

La juguetería

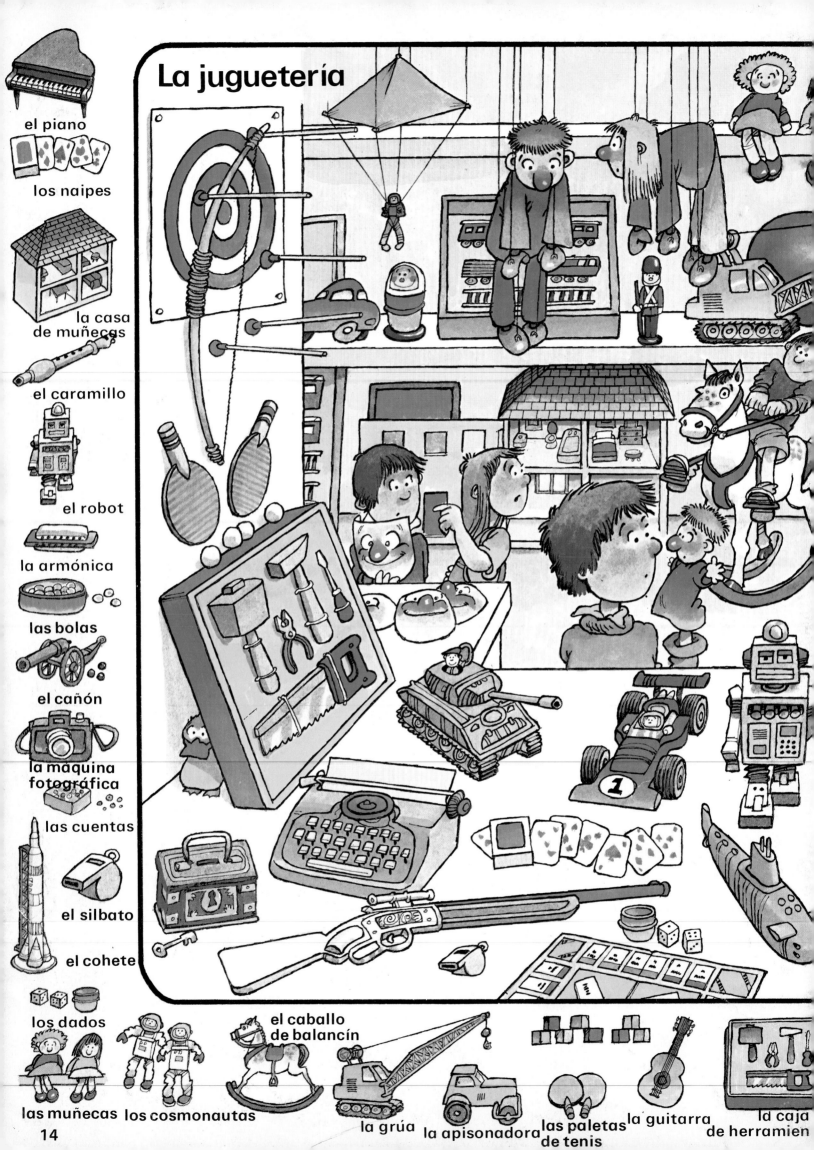

el piano

los naipes

la casa de muñecas

el caramillo

el robot

la armónica

las bolas

el cañón

la máquina fotográfica

las cuentas

el silbato

el cohete

los dados

las muñecas

los cosmonautas

el caballo de balancín

la grúa

la apisonadora

las paletas de tenis

la guitarra

la caja de herramien

14

la caña de pescar

la caja de pinturas

la arcilla

el paracaídas

la máquina de escribir

el yate

el blanco

el tanque

los soldaditos de plomo

el fuerte

la hucha

la caja de tren

los títeres

los tambores

las pelotas

el coche de carreras

las máscaras

la trompeta

el arco y las flechas

la escopeta

el submarino

15

la pelota

la cuerda

el hoyo de arena

el picnic

la cometa

el helado

el perro

los columpios

la verja

el sendero

los renacuajos

El parque

el tobogán

la rana

el matorral

los patines de ruedas

los niños

el patinete

16

los cisnes

el bebé

la tierra

las vallas

la sillita de ruedas

las palomas

el columpio

las flores

el charco

los patitos

la cuerda de saltar

el barquito

el macizo de flores

el banco

el lago

la correa de perro

los patos

los árboles 17

En el zoo

el panda

el murciélago

el pingüino

el hipopótamo

las patas

el canguro

el ala

el águila

las plumas

el avestruz

el lobo

el mono

el pelícano

la jirafa

el gorila

el oso

el castor

el león

los cachorros de león

el cocodrilo

18

los cuernos

el ciervo

el camello

la foca

los monos

el oso blanco

la trompa

el elefante

la zebra

el búfalo

el rinoceronte

el rabo

el tiburón

el delfín

el leopardo

las cabras

el tigre

la ballena

La estación de ferrocarril

El garaje

los raíles

el jefe de estación

la máquina

los topes

el vagón restaurante

los vagones

el maquinista

el tren de mercancías

el andén

las señales

el revisor

las maletas

las luces delanteras

la aceitera

el motor

la batería

el camión de gasolina

20

El aeropuerto

la azafata

el helicóptero

la pista de aterrizaje

el avión

la torre de control

el piloto

el lavado de coches

el portaequipajes

la bomba de aire

la rueda

el neumático

la llave inglesa

el capó

la grúa

el aceite

el surtidor de gasolina

21

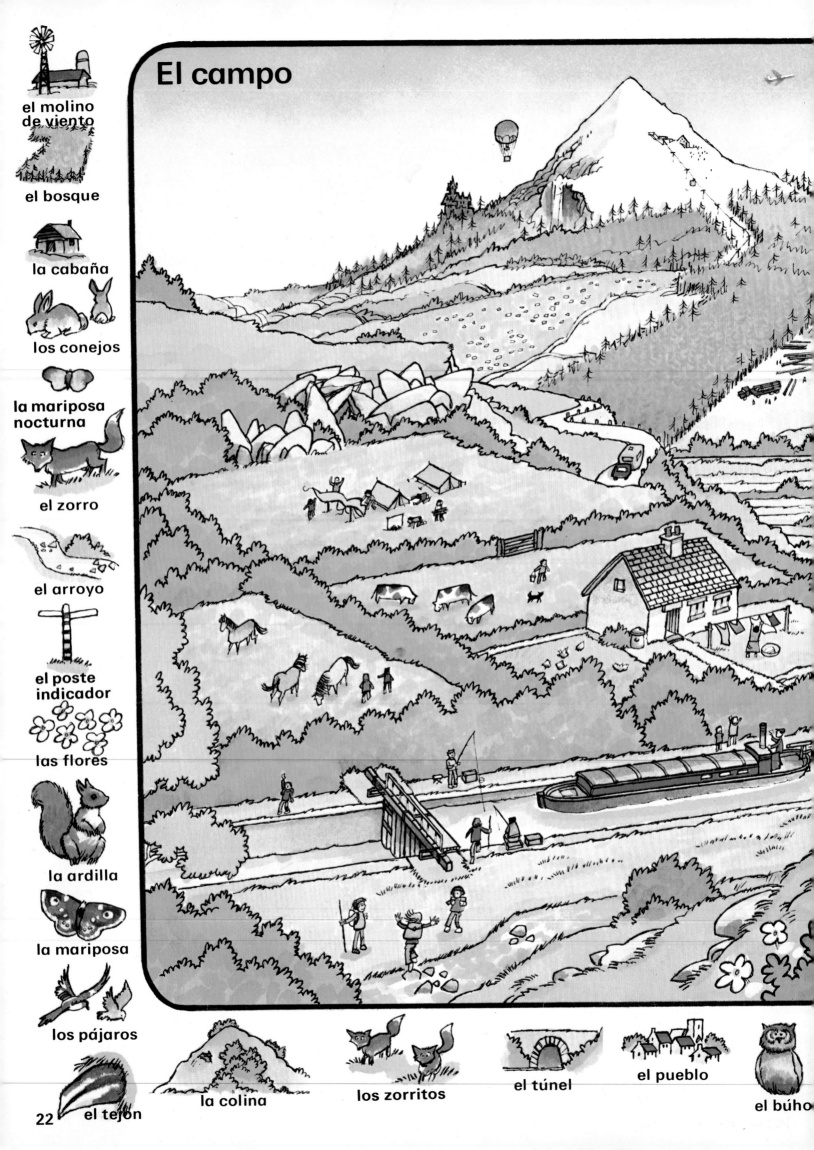

El campo

el molino de viento

el bosque

la cabaña

los conejos

la mariposa nocturna

el zorro

el arroyo

el poste indicador

las flores

la ardilla

la mariposa

los pájaros

el tejón

la colina

los zorritos

el túnel

el pueblo

el búho

22

el globo

la caravana

los troncos

las tiendas de campaña

la carretera

el puente

la barcaza

la cascada

la montaña

las piedras

el topo

la puerta de esclusa

el pescador

las rocas

el canal

el tren

el río

23

La granja

el estanque

las ovejas

el almiar

los patos

el remolque

los corderos

la valla

el pajar

la pocilga

el toro

el lodo

los cerditos

el granero

la cuadra

el granjero

la carreta

el pony

el tractor

la silla de montar

las ocas

las balas de paja

los sacos

24

el camión

el huerto

el gallinero

el establo

la vaca

los patitos

el gallo

el ternero

el arado

el perro pastor

el pastor

los pavos

el espantapájaros

la granja

los gallinas

los cerdos

los pollitos

el caballo

los ansarinos

el campo

el heno

el trigo

25

La playa

el barco de vela

el mar

el remo

el faro

la pala

el cubo

la estrella de mar

el castillo de arena

la gaviota

la bandera

el cangrejo

el marinero

el sombrero de paja

la boya

la isla

el puerto

la tumbona

la lancha de motor

el esquiador acuático

las olas

la concha
de mar

el acantilado

el barco

la canoa

las
piedrecitas

el balón

las rocas

las aletas

el alga

la red

el canalete

la barca
de pesca

el quitasol

el burro

el petrolero

el bote de remos

el traje
de baño

la cuerda

La escuela

la pecera

la placa

el techo

los lápices

los chicos

el calendario

la pared

la papelera

las tijeras

4+2 =
3−2 =

las cuentas

la regla

el pupitre

las fotos

las pinturas   el papel   los pinceles   la campanilla

a b c ch d e f
g h i j k l ll m
n ñ o p q r rr s
t u v w x y z

el abecedario

las cajas

los libros

28

a b c ch d e f g h i
j k l ll m n ñ o p q
rr r s t u v w x y z

el cuadro

las plumas

la tiza

el caballete

el suelo

las plantas

las chicas

el globo
terráqueo

la cola

el pomo de
la puerta

el cuaderno

las chinchetas

el dibujo

el mapa

los lápices
de colores

la lámpara

la pizarra

la persiana

la goma

la profesora

29

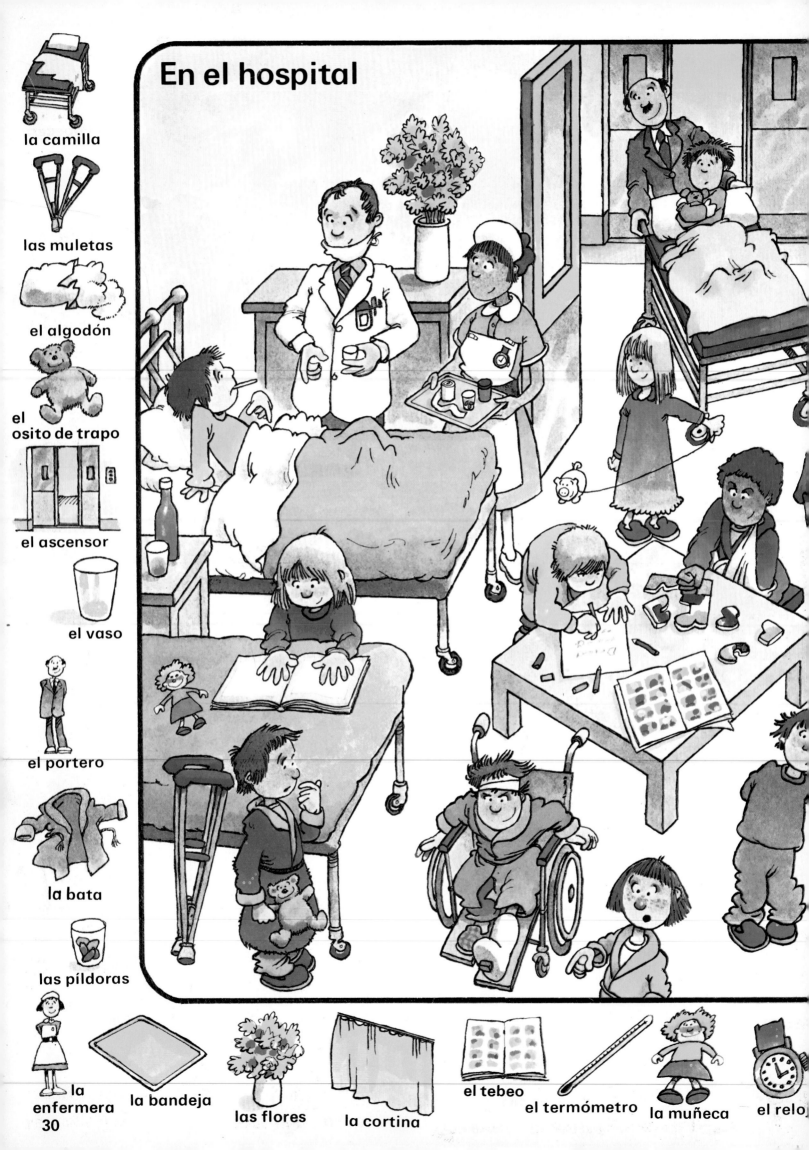

En el hospital

la camilla

las muletas

el algodón

el osito de trapo

el ascensor

el vaso

el portero

la bata

las píldoras

la enfermera

la bandeja

las flores

la cortina

el tebeo

el termómetro

la muñeca

el reloj

30

el armario
de cabecera

las medicinas

las zapatillas

el pijama

la inyección

el zumo

el camisón

el armario

la televisión

la cama

la gráfica de temperaturas

el enyesado

la venda

el ojo
morado

la silla de ruedas

el rompecabezas

el médico

31

La fiesta

los globos

las bengalas

los sombreros
de papel

el dulce
de crema

los bocadillos

la luna

los caramelos

las galletas

32

el mantel

los discos

el pastel

el chocolate

los bollos

la linterna

los juguetes

la cinta

las velas

las pajitas

las estrellas

los paquetes

el budín

los regalos

la ventana

la jalea

los fuegos artificiales

la guirnalda de papel

el disfraz

33

los plátanos
las toronjas
la lechuga
las uvas
la coliflor
las manzanas
las zanahorias
los puerros
la calabaza
el pepino
los limones
el apio
las judías
las cerezas
los albaricoques
la col
el melón

El supermercado

QUESO

CARNE

FRUTA

FRUTA

VERDURAS

los champiñones
los tomates
los guisantes
las ciruelas
las frambuesas
las cebollas
los melocotones
la piña
las patatas
las espinacas

34

PESCADO

PAN

COMESTIBLES

las latas

el pan

la mantequilla

el queso

el pollo

los huevos

el pescado

la harina

la compota

la carne

las salchichas

el yogur

el cesto

las botellas

les de Bruselas

las naranjas

las fresas

las bolsas

la caja

la balanza

el dinero

el monedero

el carrito

el bolso

35

Los alimentos

el desayuno

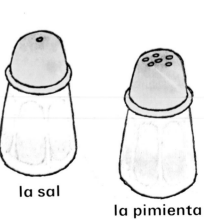

la comida

el café

el pollo

la mermelada

los huevos fritos

la leche

la miel

el chocolate caliente

las chuletas

la crema

la cerveza

el jamón

la sal

la pimienta

le cena

el té

el zumo de naranja

las nueces

la carne

el azúcar

la sopa

la tortilla

la ensalada

el cocido

las tortitas

los panecillos

el arroz

el vino

los fideos

la salsa

El cuerpo humano

el pelo

la ceja

el ojo

la nariz

la mejilla

la boca

los labios

los dientes

la lengua

la barbilla

el cuello

las orejas

la cabeza

la cara

los hombros

los brazos

el codo

las manos

los dedos

los pulgares

la espalda

el trasero

el pecho

el estómago

las rodillas

los dedos del pie

el talón

las piernas

los pies

Los vestidos

los calzoncillos

la camiseta

los pantalones

los tejanos

la camiseta

la falda

la camisa

la corbata

los pantalones cortos

los calcetines

el suéter

el jersey

la chaqueta

las medias

la blusa

el vestido

las zapatillas
de goma

los zapatos

las sandalias

las botas

los guantes

la americana

el anorak

el abrigo

el pañuelo

la gorra

el sombrero

el cinturón

los botones

los ojales

los bolsillos

la cremallera

las hebillas

los cordones

la bufanda

La gente

el actor

el cocinero

la bailarina

el submarinista

el astronauta

el director de orquesta

el carpintero

el payaso

el soldado

el policía

el granjero

la cantante

el tendero

el corredor automovilista

el mecánico

el artista

40

el bombero

el carnicero

el cartero

el buzo

el maquinista

el pintor

el alpinista

el dentista

el piloto

el juez

el guardián del zoo

el panadero

La familia

el padre
el esposo

la madre
la esposa

la hija
la hermana

el hijo
el hermano

la tía

el tío

el primo

la abuela

el abuelo

Palabras de acción

sonreir

llevar

bañarse

escribir

pensar

andar a gatos

construir

partir

pintar

romper

leer

lavarse los dientes

escuchar

cortar

caerse

lavarse

esconderse

beber

barrer

lllorar

reirse

hacer punto

bailar

atrapar

estar sentados

hacer pompas

trepar

jugar

cocinar

pelear

dormir

saltar

coseinar

esperar

mirar

lanzar

hablar

tomar

comer

coser

tirar

cavar

cantar

ganar

correr

saltar

estar de pie

hacer

comprar

andar

empujar

43

Palabras opuestas

bueno

malo

pequeño

grande

gordo

delgado

mitad

todo

frío

caliente

arriba

abajo

blando

duro

primero

último

pocas

muchas

cerca

lejos

vacío

lleno

a la izquierda

alto

bajo

sucio

limpio

44

lento

rápido

fácil

difícil

largo

corto

arriba

abajo

bonito

feo

encima

debajo

la parte delantera

la parte trasera

vivo

muerto

mojado

seco

oscuro

claro

abierto

cerrado

a la derecha

viejo

nuevo

fuera

dentro

Palabras de libros de cuentos

el castillo

el dragón

el caballero

la escoba

la bruja

la pistola

el gigante

el cañón

el pirata

el tesoro

la varita mágica

el pozo

la seta

el hada

el duende

el enano

el mago

el desierto

el ladrón

el indio

el sheriff

el vaquero

la diligencia

el demonio

la corona

el paje

la princesa

la espada

el príncipe

la reina

el rey

el palacio

el ángel

el dinosaurio

la cárcel

los renos

el trineo

el Papá Noel

el mago

la boda

el fantasma

el novio   la novia

las damas
de honor

el monstruo

47

Animales favoritos

los conejos

el gato

el perro

los peces

los lagartos

el loro

las ranas

los periquitos

el erizo

los gusanos de seda

el hámster

los sapos

los cachorros

las palomas

los ratones

las culebras

los gatitos

la tortuga

Palabras sobre el tiempo

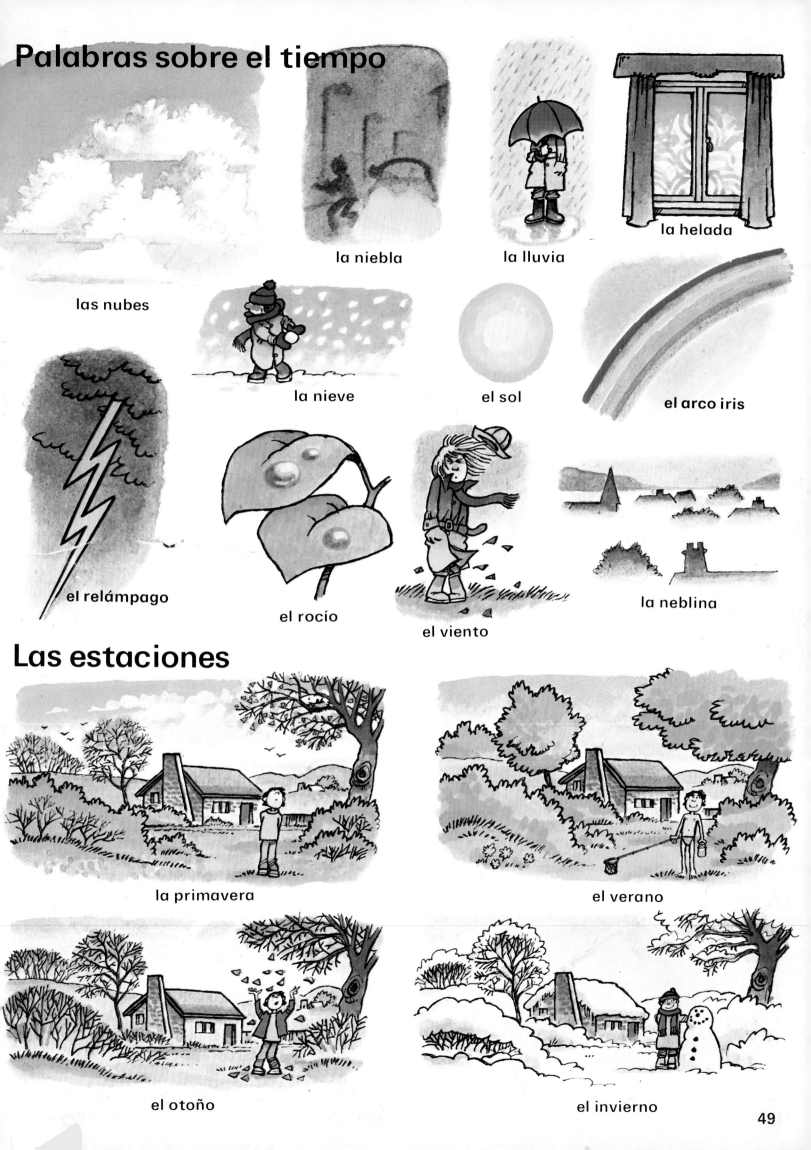

la niebla

la lluvia

la helada

las nubes

la nieve

el sol

el arco iris

el relámpago

el rocío

el viento

la neblina

Las estaciones

la primavera

el verano

el otoño

el invierno

Los deportes

el boxeo

el ciclismo

el béisbol

la natación

el fútbol

la gimnasia

el salto de altura

el esquí

la carrera de coches

el tenis

la carrera de caballos

el patinaje

el tiro al blanco

el cricket

el levantamiento de pesos

el concurso hípico

la carrera de motocicletas

la equitación

la navegación

el ping-pong

el remo

la lucha libre

el baloncesto

el judo

Los colores

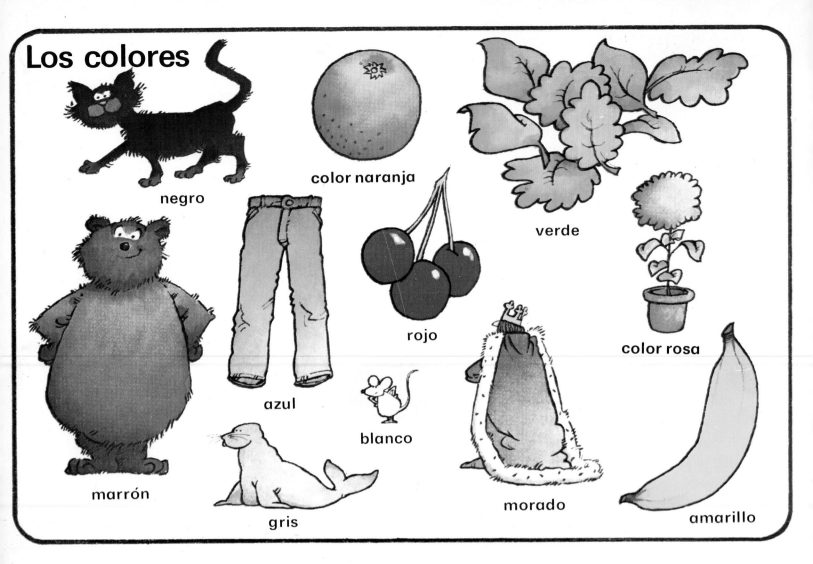

negro

color naranja

verde

marrón

azul

rojo

color rosa

blanco

gris

morado

amarillo

Las formas

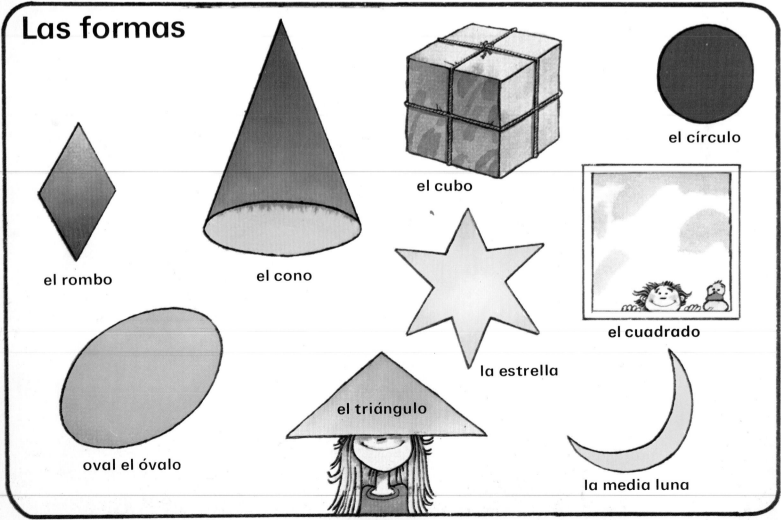

el rombo

el cono

el cubo

el círculo

la estrella

el cuadrado

oval el óvalo

el triángulo

la media luna

52

Los números

1	uno	
2	dos	
3	tres	
4	cuatro	
5	cinco	
6	seis	
7	siete	
8	ocho	
9	nueve	
10	diez	
11	once	
12	doce	
13	trece	
14	catorce	
15	quince	
16	dieciséis	
17	diecisiete	
18	dieciocho	
19	diecinueve	
20	veinte	

53

La feria

el tiovivo

la esterilla

el tobogán

la noria

los coches de choque

la montaña rusa

los aros

las palomitas de maiz

el caramelo americano

el tren fantasma

la barraca de tiro al blanco

El circo

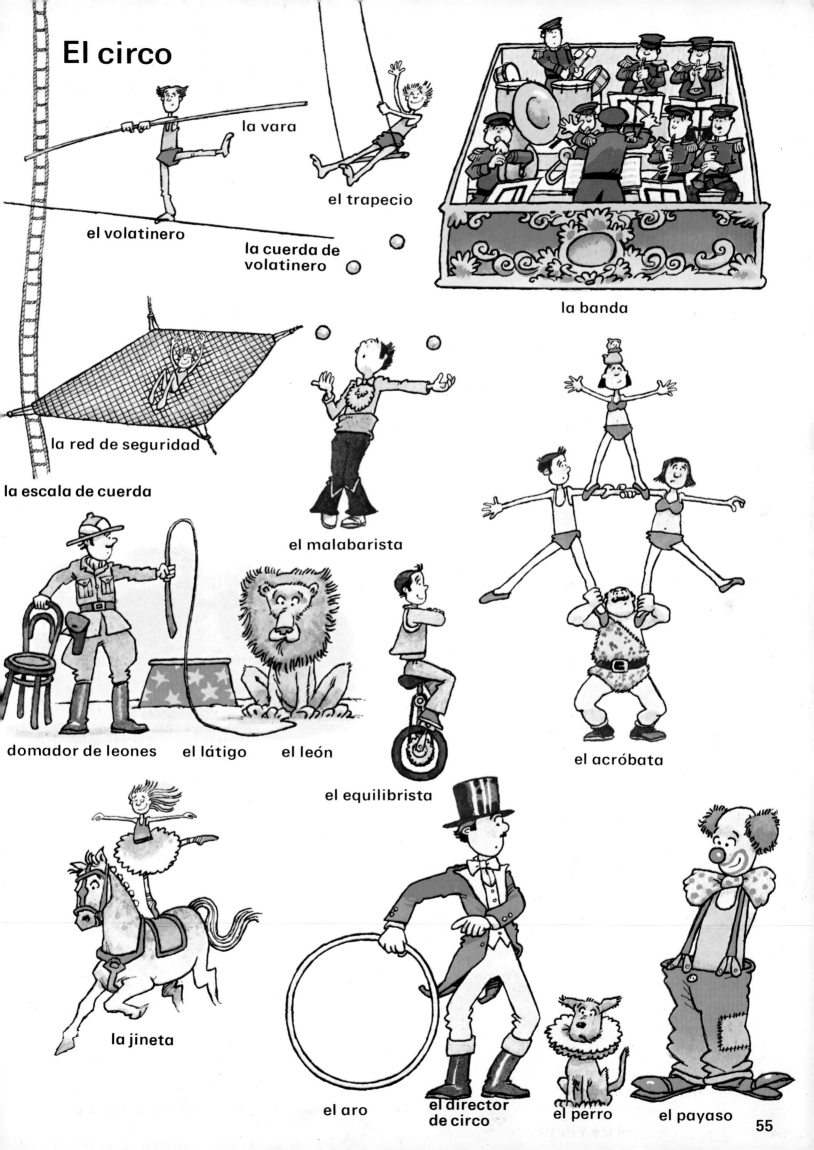

la vara

el trapecio

el volatinero

la cuerda de volatinero

la banda

la red de seguridad

la escala de cuerda

el malabarista

domador de leones

el látigo

el león

el equilibrista

el acróbata

la jineta

el aro

el director de circo

el perro

el payaso

Index   Words in the pictures

This is the alphabetical list of all the words in the pictures in this book. The Spanish word comes first, then there is the pronunciation in *italics*, followed by the English translation.

Although some Spanish words look a little like English ones, they are not pronounced in the same way. In Spanish, when the letter *c* comes before *i* or *e* it sounds like English *th* in *the*.

There are some sounds in the Spanish language which are quite different from any sounds in English. The pronunciation is a guide to help you

say the Spanish words correctly. They may look funny or strange. Just read them as if they are English words, except for these special rules:

ah is said like *a* in *tar*
eh is like *e* in *get*
ee is like *ee* in *feet*
oh is like *o* in *toe*
oo is like *oo* in *pool*
r is made by a flap of the tip of your tongue on the top of your mouth.
rr is said in the same way as a Scotsman rolls the *rr* in the word *merry*.

Spanish	Pronunciation	English
abajo	*ah-bah-gho*	bottom
el abecedario	*el ah-beh-theh-dah-ree-o*	alphabet
la abeja	*lah ah-beh-ghah*	bee
abierto/abierta	*ah-byehr-toe/ ah-byehr-tah*	open
el abrigo	*el ah-bree-go*	coat
la abuela	*lah ah-bweh-lah*	grandmother
el abuelo	*el ah-bweh-lo*	grandfather
el acantilado	*el ah-kahn-tee-lah-tho*	cliff
el aceite	*el ah-theh-ee-teh*	oil
la aceitera	*lah ah-theh-ee-teh-rah*	oil can
la acera	*lah ah-theh-rah*	pavement
el acróbata	*el ah-kro-bah-tah*	acrobat
el actor	*el akt-or*	actor
el aeropuerto	*el ah-ee-ro-pwer-toe*	airport
el agua	*el ah-gwah*	water
el águila	*el ah-gee-lah*	eagle
el agujero	*el ah-goo-gheh-ro*	hole
la ala	*lah ah-lah*	wing
el albaricoque	*el al-bah-ree-ko-keh*	apricot
las aletas	*lahs ah-leh-tahs*	flippers
la alfombra	*lah ahl-foam-bra*	carpet
la alfombrilla	*lah ahl-foam-bree-yah*	rug
el alga	*el ahl-gah*	seaweed
el algodón	*el ahl-go-dohn*	cotton wool
los alimentos	*lohs ah-lee-men-tose*	food
el almiar	*el ahl-mee-yahr*	haystack
el almohada	*el ahl-moh-ah-thah*	pillow
el alpinista	*el ahl-pee-nees-tah*	mountaineer
alto/alta	*ahl-toe/ahl-tah*	high
amarillo	*ah-mah-ree-lyo*	yellow
la ambulancia	*lah ahm-boo-lahn-thee-yah*	ambulance
la americana	*lah ah-meh-ree-kah-nah*	jacket
andar	*ahn-dar*	to walk
andar a gatos	*ahn-dar ah gah-tohs*	to crawl
el andén	*el ahn-then*	platform
el ángel	*el ahn-ghel*	angel
el animal favorito	*el ah-nee-mahl fah-boh-ree-toe*	pet
el anorak	*el ah-noh-rahk*	anorak
el ansarino	*el ahn-sah-ree-noh*	gosling
la antena de televisión	*lah ahn-teh-nah-deh teh-leh-bee-thyone*	aerial
el apio	*el ah-pee-yo*	celery

Spanish	Pronunciation	English
la apisonadora	*lah ah-pee-soh-nah-doh-rah*	steamroller
el arado	*el ah-rah-doe*	plough
la araña	*lah ah-rah-nya*	spider
el árbol	*el ahr-bole*	tree
la arcilla	*lah ar-thee-lyah*	clay
el arco	*el ahr-koh*	bow
el arco iris	*el ahr-koh ee-reese*	rainbow
la ardilla	*lah ar-dee-lyah*	squirrel
el armario	*el ar-maryo*	cupboard
el armario de cabecera	*el ahr-mah-ee-yo deh cah-beh-theh-rah*	bedside locker
la armónica	*lah armoh-nee-kah*	mouthorgan
el aro	*el ah-ro*	hoop
los aros	*los ah-rohs*	hoop-la
arriba	*ah-ree-bah*	top, upstairs
el arroyo	*el ah-roy-yo*	stream
el arroz	*el ah-rothe*	rice
el artista	*el ar-tee-stah*	artist
el ascensor	*el ahs-then-sore*	lift
el aspirador	*el ahs-pee-rah-door*	vacuum cleaner
el astronauta	*el ahs-troh-now-tah*	astronaut
atrapar	*ah-trah-pahr*	to catch
el autobús	*el ah-oo-toe-boos*	bus
el avestruz	*el ah-beh-stroos*	ostrich
el avión	*el ah-byone*	plane
la avispa	*lah ah-bees-pah*	wasp
la azada	*lah ah-thah-dah*	hoe
la azafata	*lah ah-thah-fah-tah*	air hostess
el azúcar	*el ah-thoo-kar*	sugar
azul	*ah-thool*	blue
el azulejo	*el ah-thoo-leh-ghoh*	tile
bailar	*bah-ee-lar*	to dance
la bailarina	*lah bah-ee-lahr-een-ah*	dancer
bajo/baja	*bah-ghoe/bah-ghah*	low
la bala de paja	*lah bah-lah deh paj-ghah*	straw bale
la balanza	*lah bah-lahn-thah*	scales
el balón	*el bah-lone*	balloon, ball
el baloncesto	*el bah-lone-thes-toe*	basketball
la ballena	*lah bah-yeh-nah*	whale
bañarse	*bah-nyar-say*	to bath
el banco	*el bahn-ko*	seat, bench
la banda	*la bahn-dah*	band

Spanish	Pronunciation	English
la bandeja	la bahn-deh-ghah	tray
la bandera	la bahn-deh-rah	flag
el baño	el bah-nyo	bath
el bar	el bahr	café
la barbilla	lah bahr-bee-lyah	chin
la barcaza	lah bahr-kah-thah	barge
el barco	el bahr-ko	boat
la barca de pesca	lah bahr-kah deh pehs-kah	fishing boat
el barco de vela	el bahr-ko deh beh-lah	sailing boat
el barquito	el bahr-kee-toh	toy boat
la barraca de tiro el blanco	lah bahr-rah-kah deh tee-ro el blahn-ko	rifle range
barrer	bah-rehr	to sweep
el barril	el bah-reel	barrel
la basura	lah bah-soo-rah	rubbish
la bata	lah bah-tah	dressing gown
la bateria	lah bah-teh-ree-ah	battery
el bebé	el beh-beh	baby
beber	beh-behr	to drink
la biblioteca	lah bee-blee-yoh-teh-kah	bookcase
la bicicleta	lah bee-thee-kleh-tah	bicycle
el béisbol	el beh-yeese-bole	baseball
la bengala	lah ben-gah-lah	sparkler
blanco/blanca	blahn-ko/blahn-kah	white
el blanco	el blahn-ko	target
blando/blanda	blahn-doe/blahn-dah	soft
la blusa	lah bloo-sah	blouse
la boca	lah boh-kah	mouth
el bocadillo	el boh-kah-dee-lyo	sandwich
la boda	lah boh-dah	wedding
la bola	lah boh-la	marble
el bollo	el boy-yo	bun
la bolsa	lah bole-sah	bag
el bolsillo	el bole-see-lyo	pocket
el bolso	el bole-so	handbag
la bomba de aire	lah bohm-bah deh ah-ee-ray	air pump
el bombero	el bowm-beh-ro	fireman
la bombilla	lah bowm-bee-lyah	light bulb
bonito/bonita	boh-nee-toe/boh-nee-tah	nice
el bosque	el bohs-keh	wood, forest
las botas	lahs boh-tahs	boots
el bote de pintura	el boh-teh deh peen-too-rah	paint pot
el bote de remos	el boh-te deh reh-mos	rowing boat
la botella	lah boh-teh-yah	bottle
el botón	el boh-tone	button
el boxeo	el bok-say-yo	boxing
la boya	lah boy-ya	buoy
el brazo	el brah-tho	arm
la bruja	lah broo-ghah	witch
el budín	el boo-deen	pudding
bueno/buena	bweh-noh/bweh-nah	good
el búfalo	el boo-fah-lo	buffalo
la bufanda	lah boo-fahn-dah	scarf
el buho	el boo-oh	owl
la burbúja	lah boor-boo-ghah	bubble
el burro	el boo-ro	donkey
el buzo	el boo-thoh	deep-sea diver
el caballete	el kah-bah-lyeh-teh	easel
el caballero	el kah-bah-lyeh-ro	knight
el caballo	el kah-bah-lyo	horse
el caballo de balancín	el kah-bah-lyo bah-lahn-theen	rocking horse
la cabaña	la kah-bah-nyah	hut
la cabeza	lah kah-beh-thah	head
la cabra	lah kah-bra	goat
la cacerola	el kah-ther-roh-la	saucepan
el cachorro	el kah-choh-ro	puppy
el cachorro de león	el kah-choh-ro-deh leh-yone	lion cub
caerse	kah-yehr-seh	to fall
el café	el kah-feh	coffee
la caja	lah kah-ghah	cash desk, box
la caja de herramientas	lah kah-ghah deh eh-rah-myen-tahs	tool box
la caja de pinturas	lah kah-ghah deh peen-too-rahs	paint box
la caja de tren	lah kah-ghah deh trehn	train set
el cajón	el kah-ghone	drawer
la calabaza	lah kah-lah-bah-thah	pumpkin
el calcetín	el kahl-theh-teen	sock
el calendario	el kah-len-dah-ree-yo	calendar
el calentador de agua	el kah-len-tah-dor deh ah-gwah	kettle
caliente	kah-lyen-teh	hot
la calle	lah kay-yeh	street
los calzoncillos	lohs kahl-thone-see-lyose	pants
la cama	lah kah-mah	bed
el camello	el kah-meh-lyo	camel
la camilla	lah kah-mee-lyah	trolley
el camino	el kah-mee-no	path
el camión	el kah-mee-yone	lorry
el camión de gasolina	el kah-mee-yone deh gah-so-lee-nah	petrol tanker
la camisa	lah kah-mee-sah	shirt
la camiseta	lah kah-mee-seh-tah	T-shirt, vest
el camisón	el kah-mee-sone	nightdress
la campanilla	lah kam-pah-nee-lyah	bell
el campo	el kahm-po	countryside, field
la caña de pescar	lah kah-nyah deh peh-skahr	fishing rod
el canal	el kah-nahl	canal
el canalete	el kah-nah-let-teh	paddle
el canalón del tejado	el kah-nah-lone del teh-ghah-do	gutter
el cangrejo	el kahn-greh-gho	crab
el canguro	el kahn-goo-ro	kangaroo
la canoa	lah kah-no-ah	canoe
el cañón	el kah-nyone	cannon
la cantante	lah kahn-tahn-teh	singer
cantar	kahn-tahr	to sing
el capó	el kah-po	car bonnet
la cara	lah kah-rah	face
el caracol	el kah-rah-kole	snail
el caramelo	el kah-rah-meh-lo	sweet
el caramelo americano	el kah-rah-meh-lo ah-meh-ree-kah-no	candyfloss
el caramillo	el kah-rah-mee-lyo	recorder
la caravana	lah kah-rah-bah-nah	caravan
la carcel	lah kahr-thel	prison
la carne	lah kar-neh	meat
el carnicero	el kar-nee-theh-roe	butcher
el carpintero	el kar-peen-teh-ro	carpenter
la carrera de motocicletas	lah kah-reh-rah deh moh-toh-thee-kleh-tass	speedway cycling
la carrera de caballos	lah kah-reh-rah deh kah-bah-lyose	horse racing
la carrera de coches	lah kah-reh-rah deh koh-chehs	motor racing
la carreta	lah kah-reh-tah	cart
la carretera	lah kah-reh-teh-rah	road
la carretilla	lah kah-reh-tee-lyah	wheelbarrow
el carrito	el kah-ree-toe	trolley
la carta	lah kar-tah	letter
el cartero	el kar-teh-ro	postman
la casa	lah kah-sah	house
la casa de muñecas	lah kah-sah deh moo-nyeh-kahs	dolls' house
la cascada	lah kahs-kah-dah	waterfall
el castillo	el kah-stee-lyo	castle
el castillo de arena	el kah-stee-lyo deh ah-reh-nah	sandcastle
el castor	el kah-stor	beaver
catorce	kah-tore-theh	fourteen
cavar	kah-bar	to dig
la cebolla	lah theh-bo-lyah	onion
le ceja	lah theh-ghah	eyebrow

la cena	*lah theh-nah*	supper, dinner	los comestibles	*los koh-mehs-tee-blehs*	groceries
el cepillo	*el theh-pee-lyo*	brush	la cometa	*lah koh-meh-tah*	kite
el cepillo de carpintero	*el theh-pee-lyoh deh kar-peen-teh-ro*	plane (wood)	la comida	*lah koh-mee-dah*	lunch, dinner
el cepillo de dientes	*el theh-pee-lyoh deh dyehn-tehs*	toothbrush	la cómoda	*lah koh-moh-dah*	chest-of-drawers
la cera de lustrar	*lah theh-rah deh loo-strahr*	polish	la compota	*la kohm-po-tah*	jam
cerca	*thehr-thah*	near	comprar	*kohm-prahr*	to buy
el cerdo	*el thehr-doe*	pig	la concha de mar	*lah kone-chah deh mahr*	sea shell
el cerdito	*el thehr-dee-toe*	piglet	el concurso de hípico	*el kohn-koor-soh deh ee-pee-koh*	showjumping
la cereza	*lah theh-reh-thah*	cherry	el conductor	*el kone-dook-tore*	driver
la cerilla	*lah theh-ree-lyah*	match	el conejo	*el kone-eh-gho*	rabbit
cerrado/cerrada	*theh-rah-doh/ theh-rah-dah*	shut	el cono	*el koh-no*	cone
la cerveza	*lah thehr-beh-thah*	beer	construir	*kone-stroo-eer*	to build
el cesto	*el thehs-toe*	basket	la corbata	*lah kor-bah-tah*	tie
el champiñón	*el chomp-ee-nyon*	mushroom	el cordero	*el kor-deh-ro*	lamb
la chaqueta	*lah chah-keh-teh*	cardigan	el cordón	*el kore-done*	shoelace
el charco	*el chahr-ko*	puddle	la corona	*lah koh-roh-nah*	crown
la chica	*lah chee-kah*	girl	la correa de perro	*lah koh-ray-yah deh peh-ro*	dog lead
el chico	*el chee-ko*	boy	el corredor de automotovilista	*el koh-reh-door deh ah-oo-toe-moh-toh-bee-lee-stah*	racing driver
la chimenea	*lah chee-mee-neh-ah*	chimney			
la chincheta	*lah cheen-cheh-tah*	drawing pin	correr	*koh-rehr*	to run
el chocolate	*el choh-koh-lah-teh*	chocolate	el cortacésped	*el kohr-tah-thehs-ped*	lawn mower
el chocolate caliente	*el choh-koh-lah-teh kah-lyen-teh*	hot chocolate	cortar	*kore-tahr*	to cut
			coseinar	*koh-thee-nahr*	to pick (harvest)
la chuleta	*lah choo-leh-tah*	chop	la cortina	*lah kor-tee-nah*	curtain
el ciclismo	*el thee-cleese-moh*	cycling	corto/corta	*kor-toe/kor-tah*	short
el ciervo	*el thyehr-bo*	deer	coser	*koh-sehr*	to sew
cinco	*theen-koh*	five	el cosmonauto	*kohs-moh-nah-oo-toe*	spaceman
el cine	*el thee-neh*	cinema	la crema	*lah kreh-mah*	cream
la cinta	*lah theen-tah*	ribbon	la cremallera	*lah kre-mah-yeh-rah*	zip
la cinta de medir	*lah theen-tah deh meh-deer*	tape measure	el cricket	*el kree-keht*	cricket (sport)
			el cuaderno	*el kwah-dehr-no*	notebook
el cinturón	*el theen-too-rone*	belt	la cuadra	*lah kwa-drah*	stable
el circo	*el theer-ko*	circus	el cuadro	*el kwah-dro*	picture
el círculo	*el theer-koo-loh*	circle	el cuadradro	*el kwah-dra-droh*	square
la ciruela	*lah theer-roo-eh-lah*	plum	cuatro	*kwah-tro*	four
el cisne	*el thees-neh*	swan	el cubo	*el koo-bo*	bucket, block, cube
claro/clara	*klah-roh/klah-rah*	light	el cubo de basura	*el koo-bo deh bah-soo-rah*	rubbish bin
el clavo	*el klah-boh*	nail			
el cobertizo	*el koh-behr-tee-thoh*	shed	la cuchara	*lah koo-chah-rah*	spoon
el coche	*el koh-cheh*	car	la cuchara de madera	*lah koo-chah-rah deh mah-deh-rah*	wooden spoon
el coche bomberos	*el koh-cheh bohm-beh-rohs*	fire engine	el cuchillo	*el koo-chee-lyo*	knife
el coche de carreras	*el koh-cheh deh kah-reh-rahs*	racing car	el cuello	*el kweh-lyo*	neck
			la cuenta	*lah kwen-tah*	bead, sum
los coches de choque	*lohs koh-chehs-deh choh-keh*	dodgems	la cuerda	*lah kwehr-dah*	rope
			la cuerda de saltar	*lah kwehr-dah deh sal-tahr*	skipping rope
el coche de policía	*el koh-cheh deh poh-lee-thee-yah*	police car	la cuerda de volatinero	*lah kwehr-dah deh bohl-lah-teen-er-roh*	tightrope
el cochecito de niño	*el koh-cheh-thee-toe deh nee-nyo*	pram	el cuerno	*el kwehr-no*	horn
			el cuerpo humano	*el kwehr-po oo-ma-noh*	body
el cocido	*el koh-thee-doe*	stew	la culebra	*lah koo-leh-brah*	snake
la cocina	*lah koh-thee-nah*	kitchen, cooker			
cocinar	*koh-thee-nahr*	to cook			
el cocinero	*el koh-thee-neh-ro*	cook	el dado	*el dah-doe*	dice
el cocodrilo	*el koh-koh-dree-lo*	crocodile	la dama de honor	*lah dah-mah-deh oh-nore*	bridesmaid
el codo	*el koh-doe*	elbow	debajo/debaja	*deh-bah-gho/ deh-bah-ghah*	under
el cohete	*el koh-weh-teh*	rocket			
el cojín	*el koh-gheen*	cushion	el dedo	*el deh-doe*	finger
la col	*lah koll*	cabbage	el dedo del pie	*el deh-doe del pyeh*	toe
la cola	*lah koh-lah*	glue	el delantal	*el deh-lahn-tahl*	apron
las coles de Bruselas	*lahs koh-lehs deh broo-seh-lahs*	Brussels sprouts	el delfín	*el dell-feen*	dolphin
			delgado	*dell-gah-doe*	thin
el colgador de ropa	*el kohl-gah-dor deh roh-pah*	peg	el demonio	*el deh-moh-nee-yoh*	demon
			el dentista	*el den-tees-tah*	dentist
la coliflor	*lah koh-lee-flohr*	cauliflower	dentro	*den-troh*	in
la colina	*lah koh-lee-nah*	hill	el deporte	*el deh-poor-teh*	sport
la colmena	*lah kohl-menah*	beehive	a la derecha	*ah lah deh-reh-chah*	right
el color	*el koh-lore*	colour	el desayuno	*el dah-sah-ee-yoo-no*	breakfast
color naranja	*koh-lore nah-rahn-ghah*	orange (colour)	el desierto	*el deh-see-yehr-toe*	desert
color rosa	*koh-lore roh-sah*	pink	el destornillador	*el des-tor-nee-lyah-door*	screwdriver
el columpio	*el koh-loom-pyo*	see-saw	el detergente	*el deh-tehr-ghen-teh*	washing powder
los columpios	*lohs koh-loom-pyos*	swings	el dibujo	*el dee-boo-gho*	drawing
comer	*koh-mehr*	to eat	diecinueve	*dee-yeh-thee-nweh-beh*	nineteen

Spanish	Pronunciation	English
dieciocho	dee-yeh-thee-oh-cho	eighteen
dieciséis	dee-yeh-thee-seh-eese	sixteen
diecisiete	dee-yeh-thee-syeh-teh	seventeen
el diente	el dyen-teh	tooth
diez	dee-yeth	ten
difícil	dee-fee-theel	difficult
la diligencia	lah dee-lee-ghen-thee-ya	stagecoach
el dinero	el dee-neh-ro	money
el dinosaurio	el dee-noh-sah-oo-ree-yo	dinosaur
el director de circo	el dee-rek-tore deh theer-ko	ringmaster
el director de orquesta	el dee-rek-tore deh or-kes-tah	conductor
el disco	el dees-ko	record
el disfraz	el dees-frath	costume
doce	doh-theh	twelve
el domador de leones	el do-mah-door deh leh-yoh-ness	lion tamer
dormir	door-meer	to sleep
dos	dose	two
el dragon	el drah-gohn	dragon
la ducha	lah doo-chah	shower
el duende	el dwehn-deh	elf
el dulce de crema	el dool-theh deh kreh-mah	trifle (pudding)
duro/dura	doo-roh/doo-rah	hard
el edredón	el eh-dreh-dohn	eiderdown
el elefante	el eh-leh-fahn-teh	elephant
empujar	ehm-pooh-ghahr	to push
el enano	el eh-nah-no	dwarf
encima	en-thee-mah	over
la enfermera	lah en-fair-meh-rah	nurse
la ensalada	lah en-sah-lah-dah	salad
el enyesado	el en-yeh-sah-doe	plaster
el equilibrista	el eh-kee-lee-bree-stah	trick cyclist, tightrope walker
la equitación	la eh-kee-tah-thyone	riding
el erizo	el eh-ree-tho	hedgehog
la escalera de mano	lah eh-skah-leh-rah deh mah-no	ladder
la escala de cuerda	lah ehs-kah-lah deh kwehr-dah	rope ladder
las escaleras	'ahs ehs-kah-leh-rahs	stairs
el escalón	el eh-skah-lone	step
la escoba	lah ehs-koh-bah	broom, broomstick
esconderse	eh-skone-dehr-seh	to hide
la escopeta	lah eh-skoh-peh-tah	gun
escribir	eh-skree-beer	to write
escuchar	eh-skoo-chahr	to listen
la escudilla	lah eh-skoo-dee-lyah	bowl
la escuela	lah eh-skweh-lah	school
la espada	lah eh-spah-dah	sword
la espalda	lah eh-spahl-dah	back
el espantapájaros	el eh-spahn-tah-pah-ghah-rohs	scarecrow
el espejo	el eh-speh-gho	mirror
esperar	eh-speh-rahr	to wait
las espinacas	lahs eh-spee-nah-kas	spinach
la esponja	lah eh-spohn-ghah	sponge
la esposa	lah eh-spoh-sah	wife
el esposo	el eh-spoh-so	husband
la espuma de baño	lah eh-spoo-mah deh bah-nyo	bubbles
el esquí	el eh-skee	ski
el esquiador acuático	el eh-skee-yah-door ah-kwa-tee-ko	water skier
el establo	el eh-stah-blo	cowshed
la estación de ferrocarril	lah eh-stah-thyone- deh feh-roh-kah-reel	railway staion
las estaciónes	lahs eh-stah-thyo-nehs	seasons
estar de pie	eh-star deh pyeh	to stand
estar sentados	eh-star sen-tah-dos	to sit
la estatua	lah eh-stah-too-ah	statue
la esterilla	lah eh-steh-ree-lya	mat
estirar	eh-stee-rahr	to pull
el estómago	el eh-stoh-mah-go	tummy
la estrella	lah eh-streh-lya	star
la estrella de mar	lah eh-streh-lya deh mahr	starfish
la excavadora	lah eks-kah-bah-doh-rah	digger
la fábrica	lah fah-bree-kah	factory
fácil	fah-seel	easy
la falda	lah fahl-dah	skirt
la familia	lah fah-mee-lyah	family
el fantasma	el fahn-tah-smah	ghost
el faro	el fah-ro	lighthouse
el farol	el fah-role	lamp post
feo/fea	feh-oh/feh-ah	nasty
la feria	lah feh-ree-yah	fairground
los fideos	lohs fee-deh-yohs	spaghetti
la fiesta	lah fyeh-stah	party
la flecha	lah fleh-chah	arrow
la flor	lah floor	flower
la foca	lah foh-kah	seal
la forma	lah for-mah	shape
la foto	lah foh-toe	photograph
la frambuesa	lah frahm-bweh-sah	raspberry
el fregadero	el freh-gah-deh-ro	sink
el fregasuelos	el freh-gah-sweh-lohs	mop
la fresa	lah freh-sah	strawberry
frio/fria	free-yoh/free-yah	cold
la fruta	lah froo-tah	fruit
el fuego	el fweh-go	fire
los fuegos artificiales	lohs fweh-gose art-ee-feeth-ee-yah-lehs	fireworks
fuera	fwehr-rah	out
el fuerte	el fwehr-teh	fort
la furgoneta	lah foor-goh-neh-tah	van
el fútbol	el foot-bole	football
la galleta	lah gah-lyeh-tah	biscuit
la gallina	lah gah-lyee-nah	hen
el gallinero	el gah-lyee-neh-roe	henhouse
el gallo	el gah-lyoh	cock
ganar	gah-nahr	to win
el garaje	el gah-rah-gheh	garage
la gasolinera	lah gah-soh-lee-neh-rah	petrol station
el gatito	el gah-tee-toe	kitten
el gato	el gah-toe	cat
la gaviota	lah gah-bee-yoh-tah	seagull
la gente	lah ghehn-teh	people
el gigante	el ghee-gahn-teh	giant
la gimnasia	lah gheem-nah-syah	gymnastics
el globo	el gloh-bo	balloon
el globo terráqueo	el gloh-boh teh-rah-keh-yo	globe
la goma	lah go-ma	rubber
gordo/gorda	gore-do/gore-dah	fat
el gorila	el go-ree-lah	gorilla
la gorra	lah goh-rah	cap
la gráfica de temperaturas	lah grah-fee-kah deh tem-peh-rah-too-rahs	temperature chart
grande	grahn-deh	big
el granero	el grah-neh-ro	barn
la granja	lah grahn-ghah	farm
el granjero	el grahn-gheh-ro	farmer
el grifo	el gree-fo	tap
gris	greese	grey
la grúa	lah groo-wah	crane, breakdown lorry
el guante	el gwahn-teh	glove
el guardián del zoo	el gwar-dee-an del thoo	zoo keeper
el guardarropa	el gwahr-dah-roh-pah	wardrobe
la guirnalda de papel	lah geer-nahl-dah deh pah-pell	paper chain
los guisantes	lohs gee-sahn-tehs	peas
la guitarra	lah gee-tah-rah	guitar

Spanish	Pronunciation	English
el gusano	el goo-sah-no	worm
el gusano de seda	el goo-sah-noh deh seh-dah	silkworm
hablar	ah-blahr	to talk
hacer	ah-thehr	to make
hacer pompas	ah-thehr pohm-pahs	to blow
hacer punto	ah thehr poon-toe	to knit
el hacha	el ah-chah	axe
el hada	el ah-dah	fairy
el hámster	el ahm-stehr	hamster
la harina	lah ah-ree-nah	flour
la hebilla	lah ah-bee-lyah	buckle
la helada	lah eh-lah-dah	frost
el helado	el eh-lah-doe	ice cream
el helicóptero	el eh-lee-kop-teh-ro	helicopter
el heno	el eh-no	hay
la hermana	lah ehr-ma-nah	sister
el hermano	el ehr-ma-no	brother
la hierba	lah yehr-bah	grass
la hija	lah ee-ghah	daughter
el hijo	el ee-gho	son
el hipopótamo	el ee-po-po-ta-mo	hippopotamus
la hoguera	lah oh-geh-rah	bonfire
la hoja	lah oh-ghah	leaf
el hombre	el ohm-breh	man
el hombro	el ohm-bro	shoulder
la horca	lah or-kah	fork
la hormiga	lah or-mee-ga	ant
el hospital	el oh-spee-tal	hospital
el hotel	el oh-tell	hotel
el hoyo de arena	el oi-yoh deh ah-rain-ah	sandpit
la hucha	lah oo-chah	money box
el huerto	el where-toe	orchard
el hueso	el wheh-so	bone
el huevo	el wheh-boh	egg
el huevo frito	el wheh-boh free-toe	fried egg
el humo	el oo-moh	smoke
la iglesia	lah ee-gleh-syah	church
el indio	el een-dee-yo	Indian
el interruptor	el een-teh-roop-tore	switch
el invernadero	el een-behr-nah-deh-roh	greenhouse
el invierno	el een-byehr-no	winter
la inyección	lah een-yeck-thyone	syringe
el irrigador	el ee-ree-gah-door	sprinkler
la isla	lah ees-lah	island
a la izquierda	ah lah eeth-kyair-dah	left
el jabón	el ghah-bone	soap
la jalea	lah ghal-eh-ah	jelly
el jamón	el ghah-mone	ham
el jardín	el ghar-deen	garden
el jefe de estación	el gheh-feh deh eh-stah-thyone	station master
el jersey	el ghehr-seh	jumper
la jineta	lah ghee-neh-tah	bare-back rider
la jirafa	lah ghee-rah-fah	giraffe
las judías	lah ghoo-dee-yahs	beans
el judo	el ghoo-doe	judo
el juez	el ghweth	judge
jugar	ghoo-gar	to play
el juguete	el ghoo-geh-teh	toy
la juguetería	lah ghoo-get-eh-ree-ya	toy shop
el labio	el lah-bee-yo	lip
el ladrillo	el lah-dree-lyo	brick
el ladrón	el lah-drone	robber
el lago	el lah-go	lake
la lámpara	lah lahm-pa-rah	light
la lana	lah lah-nah	wool
la lancha de motor	lah lahn-chah deh moh-tore	speedboat

Spanish	Pronunciation	English
lanzar	lahn-thahr	to throw
el lápiz	el lah-peeth	pencil
el lápiz de colores	el lah-peeth deh koh-lore-ehs	crayon
el lagarto	el lah-gahr-to	lizard
largo/larga	lar-go/lar-gah	long
la lata	lah lah-tah	tin
el látigo	el lah-tee-go	whip
le lavabo	el lah-bah-do	wash basin
el lavado de coches	el lah-boh-doe deh koh-chehs	car wash
la lavadora	lah lah-bah-doh-rah	washing machine
lavarse	lah-bar-seh	to wash
lavarse los dientes	lah-bar-seh lohs dyen-tehs	to clean teeth
la leche	lah leh-cheh	milk
la lechuga	lah leh-choo-gah	lettuce
leer	leh-air	to read
la leña	lah len-ya	firewood
la lengua	lah len-gwah	tongue
lejos	leh-ghoss	far
lento	len-toe	slow
el león	el leh-yone	lion
el leopardo	el leh-oh-par-do	leopard
el levantamiento de pesos	el leh-bahn-tah-myen-toe des peh-sose	weightlifting
el libro	el lee-bro	book
la lima	lah lee-mah	file
el limón	el lee-mone	lemon
limpio/limpia	leem-pyoh/leem-pyah	clean
la linterna	lah leen-tair-nah	lantern
la llave	lah yah-beh	key
la llave inglesa	lah yah-beh een-gleh-sah	spanner
lleno/llena	lyeh-no/lyeh-na	full
llevar	lyeh-bar	to carry
llorar	lyoh-rar	to cry
la lluvia	lah lyoo-bee-yah	rain
el lobo	le loh-bo	wolf
el lodo	el loh-doe	mud
el loro	el loh-ro	parrot
la lucha libre	la loo-cha lee-breh	wrestling
la luna	lah loo-nah	moon
la luz delantera	la looth-deh-lahn-teh-rah	headlights
la luz de vengala	la looth deh ben-gah-lah	firework
el macizo de flores	el mah-thee-thoh-deh floh-rehs	flowerbed
la madera	lah ma-deh-rah	wood
la madre	lah ma-dreh	mother
mágico/mágica	ma-ghee-ko/ma-ghee-kah	magic
el mago	el mah-gho	wizard, magician
el malabarista	el mah-lah-bah-ree-stah	juggler
la maleta	lah ma-leh-tah	suitcase
malo/mala	ma-loh/ma-lah	bad
la manguera	lah mahn-geh-rah	hose
la mano	lah ma-no	hand
el mantel	el man-tell	tablecloth
la mantequilla	lah man-teh-kee-lyah	butter
la manzana	lah mahn-thah-nah	apple
el mapa	el ma-pah	map
la máquina	lah mah-kee-nah	engine
la máquina de escribir	lah mah-kee-nah deh eh-skree-beer	typewriter
la máquina fotográfica	lah mah-kee-nah foh-toh-grah-fee-kah	camera
el maquinista	el mah-kee-nee-stah	engine driver
el mar	el mar	sea
el marinero	el ma-ree-neh-ro	sailor
la marioneta	lah ma-ree-yoh-net-ah	puppet
la mariposa	lah ma-ree-poh-sah	butterfly
la mariposa nocturna	lah mah-ree-poh-sah nok-toor-nah	moth
marrón	ma-rone	brown
el martillo	el mahr-tee-lyo	hammer
la máscara	lah mah-skah-rah	mask
el matorral	el mah-toh-rahl	bush

el mecánico	el meh-kah-nee-koh	mechanic	el otoño	el oh-toh-nyo	autumn
la media luna	lah meh-dyah loo-na	crescent	el óvalo	el oh-bah-loh	oval
las medias	lahs meh-dee-yahs	tights	la oveja	lah-oh-beh-ghah	sheep
las medicinas	lahs meh-dee-thee-nahs	medicine			
el médico	el meh-dee-ko	doctor	el padre	el pa-dreh	father
la mejilla	lah meh-ghee-lyah	cheek	el pajar	el pa-ghahr	loft
el melocotón	el meh-lo-koh-tone	peach	el pájaro	el pa-ghah-ro	bird
el melón	el meh-lone	melon	el paje	el pah-gheh	pageboy
el mercado	el mehr-kah-doe	market	la pajita	lah pah-ghee-tah	drinking straw
la mermelada	lah mehr-meh-lah-dah	jam	la pala	lah pa-la	spade
la mesa	lah mess-ah	table	la palabra de	lah pa-la-bra deh	action word
la mesita	lah meh-see-ta	small table	acción	ahk-theh-on	
la miel	lah myel	honey	la palabra de	lah pa-la-bra deh	story-book word
mirar	mee-rahr	to watch	libros de cuentos	lee-bross deh kwen-	
la mitad	lah mee-tahd	half		toss	
mojado/mojada	moh-ghah-doh/	wet	la palabra opuesta	lah pa-la-bra oh-	opposite word
	moh-ghah-dah			pwehs-tah	
el molino de viento	el moh-lee-noh deh	windmill	la palabra sobre	lah pa-la-bra soh-breh	weather word
	byen-toe		el tiempo	el tyem-po	
el monedero	el moh-neh-deh-ro	purse	el palacio	el pah-lah-syo	palace
el mono	el moh-no	monkey	la paleta	lah pa-leh-tah	trowel
el monstruo	el mone-stroo-oh	monster	la paleta de tenis	lah pah-leh-tah deh	bat, table tennis
la montaña	lah mone-tah-nyah	mountain		teh-nees	
la montaña rusa	lah mone-tah-nyah	big dipper	el palo	el pah-loh	stick
	roo-sah		la paloma	la pah-lo-ma	pigeon
morado/morada	moh-rah-do/moh-rah-dah	purple	las palomitas de	lahs pah-lo-mee-tahs deh	popcorn
la mosca	lah moh-skah	fly	maíz	mah-eeth	
la motocicleta	lah moh-toh-thee-	motor cycle	el pan	el pahn	bread
	kleh-tah		el panadero	el pah-nah-deh-ro	baker
el motor	el moh-tore	engine	el panda	el pahn-dah	panda
muchas	moo-chahs	a lot	el panecillo	el pah-neh-thee-lyo	roll
muerto/muerta	mwere-toe/mwere-tah	dead	los pantalones	los pahn-tah-loh-ness	trousers
la mujer	lah moo-ghair	woman	los pantalones	lohs pahn-tah-loh-ness	shorts
las muletas	lahs moo-leh-tahs	crutches	cortos	kor-tose	
la muñeca	lah moo-nyeh-kah	doll	el pañuelo	el pah-nyoo-weh-lo	handkerchief
el murciélago	el moor-thee-yeh-lah-go	bat	el Papá Noel	el pah-pah no-ell	Father Christmas
			el papel	el pah-pell	paper
el naipe	el nah-ee-peh	playing card	el papel de lija	el pah-pell deh lee-ghah	sand paper
la naranja	lah nah-rahn-ghah	orange (fruit)	la papelera	lah pah-peh-leh-rah	wastepaper
la nariz	lah nah-reeth	nose			basket
la natación	lah nah-tah-thee-yohn	swimming	el papel pintado	el pah-pell peen-tah-doh	wallpaper
la navaja	lah nah-bah-ghah	penknife	el paquete	el pah-keh-teh	parcel
la navegación	lah nah-beh-ghah-	sailing	el paracaídas	el pah-rah-kah-yee-dahs	parachute
	thee-yohn		la pared	lah pah-red	wall
la neblina	lah neh-blee-nah	mist	el parque	el par-keh	park
negro/negra	neh-groh/neh-grah	black	la parte delantera	lah par-teh deh-	front
el neumático	el neh-oo-mah-tee-ko	tyre		lahn-teh-rah	
la nevera	lah nehr-beh-rah	refrigerator	la parte trasera	lah par-teh trah-seh-rah	back
el nido de pájaro	el nee-doe deh	nest	partir	par-teer	to chop
	pa-ghah-ro		el paso de	el pah-so deh	pedestrian
la niebla	lah nyeh-blah	fog	peatones	peh-ya-tone-ess	crossing
la nieve	lah nyeh-beh	snow	la pasta de dientes	lah pah-stah deh	toothpaste
el niño	el nee-nyo	child		dyen-tess	
la noria	lah no-ree-ya	big wheel	el pastel	el pahs-tell	cake
la novia	lah no-bee-yah	bride	el pastor	el pah-store	shepherd
el novio	el no-bee-yo	bridegroom	la pata	lah pah-tah	paw
la nube	lah noo-beh	cloud	la patata	lah pah-tah-tah	potato
nueve	nweh-beh	nine	el patinaje	el pah-tee-nah-gheh	skating
nuevo/nueva	nweh-boh/nweh-bah	new	el patín de ruedas	el pah-teen deh	roller skate
la nuez	lah noo-weth	nut		roo-weh-dahs	
el número	el noo-meh-roh	number	el patinete	el pah-tee-neh-teh	scooter
			el pato	el pah-toe	duck
la oca	lah oh-kah	goose	el patio de recreo	el pah-tee-yo deh	playground
ocho	oh-cho	eight		reh-kreh-yo	
el ojal	el oh-ghahl	buttonhole	el patito	el pah-tee-toe	duckling
el ojo	el oh-gho	eye	el pavo	el pah-bo	turkey
el ojo morado	el oh-gho moh-rah-doe	black eye	el payaso	el pah-yah-so	clown
la ola	lah oh-lah	wave	la pecera	lah peh-theh-rah	aquarium
once	ohn-theh	eleven	el pecho	el peh-cho	chest
la oreja	lah oh-reh-ghah	ear	el peine	el peh-ee-neh	comb
la oruga	lah oh-roo-gah	caterpillar	pelear	peh-leh-yahr	to fight
oscuro/oscura	oh-skoo-ro/oh-skoo-rah	dark	el pelicano	el peh-lee-kah-no	pelican
el osito de trapo	el oh-see-toh deh trah-po	teddy bear	el pelo	el peh-lo	hair
el oso	el oh-so	bear	la pelota	lah peh-lo-ta	ball
el oso blanco	el oh-so blahn-koh	polar bear	pensar	pen-sahr	to think
			el pepino	el pep-pee-no	cucumber

Spanish	Pronunciation	English
pequeño/ pequeña	*peh-keh-nyoh/ peh-keh-nyah*	small
el periódico	*el peh-ree-oh-dee-koh*	newspaper
el periquito	*el peh-ree-kee-toh*	budgerigar
el perro	*el peh-ro*	dog
el perro pastor	*el peh-roh past-or*	sheep dog
la persiana	*lah pehr-see-ya-na*	window blind
el pescado	*el pess-kah-doe*	fish
el pescador	*el pess-kah-dor*	fisherman
el petrolero	*el peh-troh-leh-ro*	oil tanker
el piano	*el pyah-no*	piano
el picnic	*el peek-neek*	picnic
el pie	*el pyeh*	foot
la piedra	*lah pyeh-drah*	stone
la piedrecita	*lah pyeh-dreh-thee-tah*	pebble
la pierna	*lah pyehr-nah*	leg
el pijama	*el pee-ghah-ma*	pyjama
la píldora	*lah peel-doh-rah*	pill
el piloto	*el pee-lote-oh*	pilot
la pimienta	*lah pee-mee-yen-tah*	pepper
la piña	*lah pee-nyah*	pineapple
el pincel	*el peen-sell*	brush
el ping-pong	*el peen-pon*	table tennis
el pingüino	*el peen-gwee-no*	penguin
pintar	*peen-tahr*	to paint
el pintor	*el peen-tore*	painter
la pintura	*lah peen-too-rah*	paint
el pirata	*el pee-rah-tah*	pirate
el piso	*el pee-so*	flat
la pista de aterrizaje	*lah pee-stah deh ah-teh-ree-thah-gheh*	runway
la pistola	*la pee-stoh-lah*	pistol
la pizarra	*lah pee-thah-rah*	blackboard
la placa	*lah plah-kah*	badge
la plancha	*lah plahn-chah*	iron
la planta	*lah plahn-tah*	plant
el plátano	*el plah-tah-no*	banana
el platito	*el plah-tee-toe*	saucer
el plato	*el plah-toh*	plate
la playa	*lah plah-ee-yah*	beach, seaside
la pluma	*lah ploo-mah*	pen
la pocilga	*lah poh-theel-gah*	pig sty
pocas	*po-cahs*	little
la policía	*lah poh-lee-thee-ya*	policeman
el pollito	*el poh-lyee-toe*	chick
el pollo	*el poh-lyo*	chicken
el pomo de la puerta	*el poh-moh deh lah pwer-tah*	door handle
el pony	*el po-nee*	pony
el portaequipajes	*el poor-tah-eh-kee-pah-gheh*	boot (of car)
el portero	*el poor-tehr-oh*	porter
el poste indicador	*el poh-steh een-dee-kah-dore*	signpost
el pote	*el poh-teh*	jar
el pozo	*el po-tho*	well
la prima	*lah pree-mah*	cousin (female)
la primavera	*lah pree-mah-beh-rah*	spring
el primero	*el pree-mah-ro*	first
el primo	*el pree-mo*	cousin (male)
la princesa	*lah preen-theh-sah*	princess
el príncipe	*el preen-theeh-peh*	prince
la profesora	*lah pro-fess-or-ah*	teacher
el pueblo	*el pweh-blo*	village
el puente	*el pwen-teh*	bridge
el puerro	*el pweh-ro*	leek
la puerta	*lah pwer-tah*	door
la puerta de esclusa	*lah pwehr-tah deh eh-skloo-sah*	lock (canal)
el puerto	*el pwer-toe*	harbour
el pulgar	*el pool-gahr*	thumb
el pupitre	*el poo-pee-tray*	desk
el queso	*el keh-so*	cheese
quince	*keen-theh*	fifteen
el quitasol	*el kee-tah-sol*	umbrella
el rabo	*el rah-bo*	tail
el radiador	*el rah-dee-yah-door*	radiator
la radio	*lah rah-dee-yo*	radio
el rail	*el ray-yeel*	railway line
la rana	*lah rah-nah*	frog
rápido	*rah-pee-do*	fast
el rastrillo	*el rah-stree-lyo*	rake
el ratón	*el rah-tone*	mouse
el recogedor del polvo	*el reh-koh-gheh-dore del pole-bo*	dustpan
la red	*lah red*	net
la red de seguridad	*lah red deh seh-goo-ree-dahd*	safety net
el regalo	*el reh-gah-lo*	present
el relámpago	*el reh-lahm-pah-go*	lightning
la regla	*lah reh-glah*	ruler
la reina	*lah reh-ee-nah*	queen
reírse	*reh-eer-seh*	to laugh
el reloj	*el reh-logh*	clock, watch
el remo	*el reh-mo*	oar, rowing
el remolque	*el reh-mole-keh*	trailer
el renacuajo	*el reh-nah-kwah-gho*	tadpole
el reno	*el reh-no*	reindeer
el retrete	*el reh-treh-teh*	toilet
el revisor	*el reh-bee-sore*	ticket collector
el rey	*el reh-ee*	king
el rinoceronte	*el ree-no-theh-rohn-teh*	rhinoceros
el río	*el ree-yo*	river
el robot	*el roh-boat*	robot
la roca	*la roh-kah*	rock
el rocío	*el roh-thee-yo*	dew
la rodilla	*lah roh-dee-lyah*	knee
rojo/roja	*roh-gho/roh-ghah*	red
el rombo	*el rome-boh*	diamond
el rompecabezas	*el rome-peh-kah-beh-thahs*	jigsaw
romper	*rome-pehr*	to break
la rueda	*lah roo-weh-dah*	wheel
la sábana	*lah sah-bah-nah*	sheet
el saco	*el sah-ko*	sack
la sal	*lah sahl*	salt
la salchicha	*lah sahl-chee-chah*	sausage
la salsa	*lah sahl-sah*	sauce
saltar	*sahl-tahr*	to jump, to skip
el salto de altura	*el sahl-toh deh ahl-too-rah*	high jump
las sandalias	*lahs sahn-dah-lee-yahs*	sandals
el sapo	*el sah-po*	toad
la sartén	*lah sahr-ten*	frying pan
seco/seca	*seh-koh/seh-kah*	dry
seis	*seh-eese*	six
el semáforo	*el seh-mah-foh-roh*	traffic lights
la semilla	*lah seh-mee-lyah*	seed
la señal	*lah seh-nyal*	signal
el sendero	*el sen-deh-ro*	path
el serrín	*el seh-reen*	sawdust
la seta	*lah seh-tah*	mushroom
el seto	*el seh-toh*	hedge
el sheriff	*el sheh-reef*	sheriff
la sierra	*lah see-air-rah*	saw
siete	*syeh-teh*	seven
el silbato	*el seel-bah-toe*	whistle
la silla	*la see-lyah*	chair
la silla de montar	*lah see-lyah deh mohn-tahr*	saddle
la silla de ruedas	*lah see-lyee deh roo-weh-dahs*	wheelchair
la sillita de ruedas	*lah see-lee-tah deh roo-weh-dahs*	pushchair
el sol	*el sohl*	sun
el soldadito de plomo	*el sole-dah-dee-toh deh ploh-mo*	toy soldier
el soldado	*el sole-dah-doe*	soldier
el sombrero	*el sohm-breh-roh*	hat
el sombrero de paja	*el sohm-breh-roh deh pah-ghah*	straw hat